Bella came to one of our down with a book she had written and illustrated bu formatted.

She informed Marisha Kiddle that she had written this book, that she was only 5 years old, and that this was 'her first book'. She already had the title and plot worked out for the next one.

Her pitch was as confident as some of our adult writers, so we both agreed her book should be published. Snowy, captured our hearts and this book is an amazing achievement for such a young child … We are looking forward to Snowy's next adventure.

Diane Narraway & Marisha Kiddle

For my Mummy, Daddy
and my sister
Lacie May

love

FRIDAY JULY 1st 2022
HAPPY HAPPY HAPPY
BIRTHDAY ASHER
i hope that you have a
FANFABULOUS DAY
& lots more to come.
All my LOVE HUGS & KISSES
Sve I all my little ones.

just for you XXx's

GINGER FYRE PRESS

GINGERFYREPRESS.COM

GINGERFYREPRESS@GMAIL.COM

Typesetting Ginger Fyre Press December 2021

Ginger Fyre Press is an imprint of venoficia Publications

the lost cat
by
Bella J Dark

Once upon a time, there was a cat called Snowy.

Snowy lived at home with her mum. in a land called Cat land.

Snowy wanted to go outside. She had never been outside before, so Snowy asked her mum but her mum said no!

At night-time Snowy
went outside it was

really, really, dark.
she found a park.

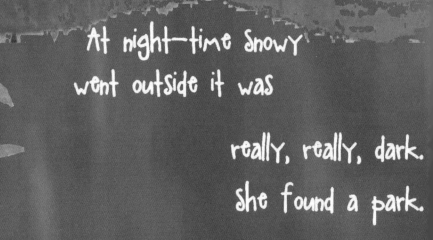

Then the
    Sun came up.

Is Snowy asleep?

No!

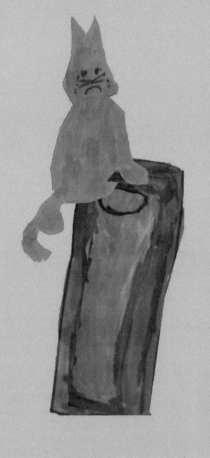

Snowy's mum is sad.
She can't find Snowy.
She is very sad.

Snowy's mum is
very, very, very, sad.

Snowy is lost.
She can't find her
way home.

Snowy misses her mum.

Snowy is very, very, very, sad.

Another mummy
        came to help Snowy.

The mum took snowy to the police.

The policeman took Snowy
to her home.

She saw her
mummy.

Snowy's mum put an alarm in her room to keep her safe.

Snowy tried to sneak outside but the alarm went off.

Snowy's mum came into her room. She said,

"The alarm is to keep you safe."

This reminded Snowy how she was

lost and scared on her own.

In the morning, Snowy watched the rain pour down while she laid in bed.

When it was sunny Snowy went outside with her mum.

She played on the swings. It was fun.

Snowy never went outside without
her mum again!!!

The End

There is another story of snowy
to come, have a good night and have a nice
weekend.

Bella x

Me and my big sister Lacie May

Picture by Lacie May

Printed in Great Britain
by Amazon

82470577R00020